THREE'S NOT
A CROWD

TAHIRIH LEMON

THREE'S NOT A CROWD

Sacred Square Publishing

CONTENTS

CONTENTS

INTRODUCTION

Surviving and navigating your teen years, including high school, can be challenging at the best of times. It is certainly easier to cope with when accompanied by your best friends.

Join Jade, a free-spirited vegetarian, Raj who is mad about science and always hungry, and Shingo, an easy-going, insightful Baha'i - through their various adventures, events, and incidents encountered throughout their junior high school years.

Three's Not a Crowd is the first in the Seekers of Truth Series. It can be read independently, however, it has been designed to initiate discussions within your junior youth (JY) group and encourage you to reflect on your personal experiences with friends and at school. Each book addresses a range of current social issues and concerns and highlights spiritual truths.

At the end of the story is a series of questions based on the concepts covered in each chapter. Additional references have been linked to The Independent Investigator Series to provide more in-depth information supported by quotes from the Baha'i Writings.

Topics covered in this book include natural and spirit forces, life after death, the soul, progressive revelation, the dual nature of man, alcohol, cyberbullying, backbiting, and the Junior Youth Empowerment Program.

LET THE HOLIDAYS BEGIN!

'We survived the first year of high school!' exclaims Jade, walking through the school's front gate alongside her best friends Shingo and Raj.

'We did,' agrees Shingo, removing his school tie. 'I'm so glad it's the school holidays.'

'Yeah,' says Raj carrying a backpack crammed with school exercise books. 'Now I have more time to work on my science experiments.'

'Ugh, Raj. Don't you ever just chill?' asks Jade gazing wide-eyed.

'That is me 'chilling',' says Raj pushing his dark brown curly hair away from his equally dark brown eyes.

'Well, I'm looking forward to sleeping in. Watching some Anime. And I get more computer time,' says Shingo.

'After New Year's Eve, I'm going on a camping trip

with my family to Fraser Island. My parents said you guys can come too,' announces Jade.

'I don't know,' responds Raj.

'Come on Raj, it will be fun,' says Shingo. 'I'll ask my parents when I get home.'

'Raj, please come,' requests Jade. 'It wouldn't be the same without you. We can sleep under the stars, which are so much brighter away from the city lights. You can even bring your telescope and stargaze.'

'I'll think about it and get back to you,' replies Raj.

'Cool,' says Jade, revealing a tooth gap-smile across her lightly freckled face. 'You won't regret it.'

*****

'I'm so glad you guys could make it. We are going to have so much fun,' exclaims Jade. Her green eyes shining with excitement, with a skip in her step climbing up the ramp onto the ferry.

'Yes, I'm glad my parents agreed to let me come. I was starting to get a bit bored after Christmas. Plus, I missed hanging out with you guys,' says Shingo, tucking as much of his straight black fringe under his cap away from his eyes.

'I must admit, I am surprised my parents agreed to let me come. They said something about, "it will do me good", to get out,' says Raj.

'Let's go sit on the upper deck, so we have a better view,' suggests Jade.

'I'm starting to feel a bit queasy,' comments Shingo.

'Oh, you might be experiencing seasickness,' says Jade. 'Here's a plastic bag, just in case. We should be there soon. You'll feel better when we're back on land.'

'So, Raj, what science experiments were you working on during the school holidays?' asks Jade.

'Well, I've been researching about the four fundamental natural forces of the universe,' replies Raj.

'What are they?' asks Shingo weakly, as the colour drains from his face, and saliva forms in his mouth.

'Only four, that's interesting. I would've thought there would've been so many more,' comments Jade.

'They are gravity, the weak force, electromagnetic force, and the strong force,' responds Raj.

'I remember learning about gravity in science this year. But I've not heard about "the weak force" or the "strong force". Sounds like something from a science fiction movie,' remarks Jade.

'I thought electricity and magnetism were two separate forces,' says Shingo.

'Yes, in the past physicists thought electricity and magnetism were two separate forces. But they discovered that in fact, they are two components of the same force,' replies Raj.

'So how exactly are they components of the same force?' asks Shingo.

'Well the electric part occurs between charged particles whether they are moving or not, creating a field in which the charges can influence each other,' explains

Raj. 'But once set in motion, those charged particles begin to reveal a magnetic force.'

'That's interesting,' says Jade. 'We'll have to continue this conversation later, as we're about to dock. So glad you managed to keep your breakfast down Shingo.'

EXPLORING THE ISLAND

'Wow look at that this place it's amazing!' exclaims Shingo. Taking in the towering cliffs of multi-coloured sand, at Cathedral Beach.

'Yes, it's beautiful. Like sculptured ribbons through-out the sand,' adds Jade. 'What are we waiting for? Let's hike up to the top.'

'Well, I'm not as fit as I thought,' puffs Raj.

'Maybe, this is why your parents thought it was a good idea for you to get outside in the great outdoors, instead of cooped up in your room,' teases Jade.

'Look at this view,' announces Shingo.

'Let me catch my breath,' gasps Raj.

'Okay,' agrees Jade, as she plonks onto her laid out towel on the hot sand.

'So, Raj tell me more about what you've learned about the forces of nature,' encourages Shingo. 'You mentioned something about a weak force and a strong force.

It does sound like something out of Star Wars, instead of science.'

'The weak force is also known as the weak nuclear interaction,' explains Raj. 'It's what's responsible for particle decay. Actually, out of the four forces, it plays a greater role in things falling apart, or decaying.'

'What about the strong force?' asks Jade.

'The strong force is also known as the strong nuclear force. It's the most powerful of the four forces,' explains Raj. 'In fact, it's six thousand trillion, trillion, trillion times stronger than the force of gravity.'

'That's a lot of trillions. How many zeroes would that be?' asks Shingo.

'Thirty-nine zeros,' replies Raj. 'It's what holds together the parts of an atom and other particles. It's like the 'glue' holding matter together.'

'That's interesting,' comments Shingo.

'Yes, and more importantly it supports my theory that I'm the stronger force within our group,' jokes Jade.

'Really?' asks Raj. 'Then what force am I and Shingo, according to your universe?'

'That's easy,' replies Jade. 'Raj you're gravity. Because you're the more serious one out of the three of us. You keep us grounded.'

'Interesting,' reflects Shingo. 'What am I? I'm certainly not a weak force.'

'You are electromagnetism. Raj and I met each other through you,' replies Jade.

'Let's go for a swim,' suggests Shingo.

'I'll race you down to the bottom. The last one in has to do the washing up tonight!' Jade calls out, as she sprints towards the beach, removing her elastic band, releasing her long red wavy hair.

*****

'This is so cool,' admits Shingo, lying between Jade and Raj tucked in their sleeping bags, just outside the family tent. 'I don't think I've ever seen so many stars in my life.'

'There's the Southern Cross,' points Raj, sitting up. 'You can also see the Centaurus Constellation. Through my telescope, you can see it's actually a triple star system.'

'Wow, the sky looks even more amazing through the telescope,' exclaims Jade.

'Did you know there's a dark nebula located near the Southern Cross, called the Coalsack Nebula?' asks Raj. 'In Aboriginal culture, it's known as the head of the emu.'

'I can see it. It does look like the head of an emu,' agrees Jade.

'I was thinking about how you said there are four natural forces for all matter,' says Shingo. 'It's interesting because there are also four spirit forces in this world.'

'Oh, I didn't know that,' comments Jade. 'What exactly do you mean by spirit forces?'

'I certainly, have never heard of spirit forces,' admits Raj. 'It doesn't sound very scientific.'

'Spirit forces are invisible just like gravity, electromagnetism, and the other natural forces. They're so real, that if for one moment they were removed, all of creation would collapse,' says Shingo. 'Spirit forces are powers radiating from God, which envelope, surround and spread through all of creation.'

'You mean like, the sun's rays?' asks Jade. 'Without the sun all of life as we know it would cease to exist on earth.'

'That's a great example,' responds Shingo.

'What are these four spirit forces?' asks Raj.

'Think of creation as having four spheres or as Baha'is call them, 'kingdoms'', explains Shingo. 'There's the mineral kingdom, the plant kingdom, the animal kingdom, and the human kingdom. Each has its own specific characteristic spirit force. Plus, each higher kingdom possesses the spirit forces of the kingdoms below it.'

'What are the characteristics of each of these so-called, kingdoms?' asks Raj.

'The mineral kingdom possesses the power of cohesion. The plant kingdom possesses the power of growth and the power of cohesion,' replies Shingo. 'The animal kingdom possesses the powers of senses – sight, hearing, smell, taste, and touch, plus the powers of growth and cohesion. The human kingdom possesses the power of the soul, as well as the power of the senses, growth, and cohesion. It's the power of our soul working through our mind that enables us to think, imagine, and create.'

'Why don't they teach us this in school?' queries Raj.

'Because at the moment many people don't recognise the harmony between science and religion. Both are truths of the same reality. Without science, religion can deteriorate to superstition and fanaticism. Without religion, science becomes a vehicle for materialism, instead of being used for the benefit of all people.'

'That makes sense,' reflects Jade. 'I like how there are four natural forces and four spirit forces. Without both, nothing would exist.'

'I'd like to learn more about these spirit forces, especially the soul. I'm not even sure, I believe in God,' states Raj.

'I believe there is a Creator, but who that is, I don't know,' admits Jade. 'My Aunt Mary was in a car accident, and "died" while in hospital. She was resuscitated and came back to life. She didn't believe in God before then but now she does. Aunt Mary says there's an Afterlife and she isn't scared to die anymore - it just wasn't her time.'

'That would've been a cool experience,' remarks Shingo.

'It's comforting knowing that when we die, we go to another world. It's like an adventure,' says Jade.

'Well, I don't know about you, but I'm beat,' announces Shingo. 'I can't believe this is our last night.'

'Yes, I'm glad I came,' adds Raj. 'Although, now I have

more things to research when I get back home. Like spirit forces and the soul.'

'I'm glad you guys came. It wouldn't have been as much fun without you both,' expresses Jade. 'Now if any of you snore, I'm going to smother you with my pillow. Goodnight.'

THE WAKE

'Where's Jade?' asks Raj. 'It's not like her to miss a Visual Arts class.' He glances at the door as other students file into the classroom.

'Her grandmother died last night. She texted, and asked me to tell you,' replies Shingo.

'That's sad. I really liked Nana Ruth,' says Raj. 'And not just for her famous chocolate chip cookies.'

'Yeah,' agrees Shingo. 'She was always happy and laughing. Made you feel like part of the family.'

'Let's stop by Jade's on the way home, and see how she's going,' suggests Raj.

'Ok. But she may be too sad, and not want to talk,' responds Shingo, as he turns to the front of the class where the teacher is patiently standing, waiting for the class to settle to begin the lesson.

*****

Jade with red, swollen eyes answers the door.

'Hi, Jade,' greets Shingo. 'We just wanted to check on you and tell you how sorry we are to hear Nana Ruth died.'

'We wanted to offer our condolences,' adds Raj.

'Thanks, guys,' says Jade. 'I still can't believe she's gone. Hasn't sunken in yet.'

'When's the funeral?' asks Shingo. 'If we're allowed, we'd like to attend and be there for you.'

'My parents are trying to organise that today. I'll let you know,' responds Jade. 'Thanks for dropping by. Sorry, I'm not really up to talking. I'll be back at school later in the week.'

'Sure, we understand,' replies Shingo.

'Again, I'm really sorry,' conveys Raj.

They turn to wave as they descend the front porch, only to see Jade has already disappeared into the house.

*****

'Your Nana Ruth was loved by so many people,' remarks Shingo, as he scans the room bulging with people of all ages, predominately dressed in black.

'Yes, she was,' agrees Jade. 'I really miss her.'

'I like how you made her famous chocolate chip cookies,' says Raj, who had already eaten one, while holding another in mid-air.

'You know I've never seen an open casket before. Or someone who has died,' comments Shingo.

'She looked so peaceful,' reflects Raj.

'Last night I dreamed she visited me,' recalls Jade. 'It seemed so real. She was glowing and happy. She told me to be happy for her - not sad.'

'It probably was her visiting you,' affirms Shingo. 'Did you know some of our dreams are proof of the existence of our soul? Like when people have *déjà vu* experiences.'

'I don't think I've ever had a *déjà vu* experience,' comments Raj.

'I haven't either,' says Shingo. 'It's comforting knowing when we die our souls continue to live and progress through all the worlds of God.'

'You just said worlds,' highlights Jade. 'I thought when people died, they went to heaven or hell, depending on if they did good things in their life or bad things, like steal and commit murder.'

'I thought you just ceased to exist, and everything went black,' says Raj.

'Well heaven and hell are not actual places, like a golden gate in the clouds or a fiery pit down below,' explains Shingo. 'They're a state of mind. You can experience feelings of heaven and hell, even in this life.'

'Why then do so many other people, especially Christians, believe heaven and hell are actual places?' asks Jade.

'Because during the time of Jesus many people were illiterate. Metaphors of heaven and hell were used to put fear into people to do the right thing and live morally,' answers Shingo. 'Many people interpret the verses and parables in The Bible literally, instead of understanding its spiritual and divine meanings.'

'What about the worlds you mentioned?' quizzes, Raj. 'You said there were many worlds of God. That sounds interesting.'

'The Baha'i Writings states there's an infinite number of worlds,' answers Shingo. 'It's really mind-blowing. It makes sense though, since our soul is immortal, and we live for all of eternity.'

'I'd like to hear more about the soul and what the next world is like, later,' asserts Jade. 'Let's grab some more chocolate chip cookies before they all disappear.'

'I can't argue with that logic,' agrees Raj, brushing the crumbs off his shirt.

PIZZA & MOVIE NIGHT

'Thanks for inviting us over for pizza and movie night,' says Jade, sitting back comfortably on the cushioned outdoor chair, petting Buster, Shingo's Golden Retriever. 'It's been very quiet and sombre at our place. We're all missing Nana Ruth terribly.'

'Yes, this was a great idea,' agrees Raj, as he reaches for another piece from the outdoor table covered in pizza boxes. 'I especially love this Meat Lover's pizza.'

'I'm more of a Supreme fan with the lot,' declares Shingo.

'I'm enjoying this vegetarian pizza,' says Jade. 'What movie are we watching?'

'I wanted us to watch a movie about the Afterlife, but my parents wouldn't allow me to download any of the ones I wanted because of their ratings,' sighs Shingo. 'So, I hope you don't mind we're watching the movie *Coco*. It's animated.'

'Ooh, I always wanted to watch *Coco*,' exclaims Jade. 'I heard it's good.'

'I like animated movies,' states Raj.

*****

'I never knew Halloween was celebrated in Mexico as the Day of the Dead,' reflects Jade. 'I like how they show love and respect to their ancestors, believing this will influence them in the Afterlife.'

'That's why it's important to pray for family and friends who've died,' remarks Shingo. 'Our prayers and giving charity in their name will assist their souls to progress in the next world. We should pray for them, as they pray for us.'

'So where exactly is this next world and what is it like?' questions Raj.

'The Baha'i Writings tell us the next world is connected to this physical world. In fact, there's no real separation,' answers Shingo. 'A useful analogy is this stone exists, but it's not aware that this palm tree, Buster and we exist and are sitting right next to it. Just because it's not aware of our existence, it doesn't mean we don't exist. All objects and living things are at different levels within this world.'

'So, people who have psychic abilities are able to see the next world, but most people can't until they die?' asks Jade.

'Yes, some can perhaps see a glimpse of the next

world or interact with spiritual beings. Although this is viewed as a gift, people with psychic abilities are not encouraged to develop these further, because they don't truly understand their effects and may unintentionally cause harm,' says Shingo. 'The next world is described as a world of lights. Obviously, not like in the movie, which was also colourful and bright. The next world is so bright, that this physical world in comparison, is like its shadow.'

'So, when you die, do you reunite with family and friends who have already died?' queries Raj.

'Definitely, although you won't be in your physical body anymore, but you retain your individuality and other souls you loved in this life will recognise and greet you,' explains Shingo. 'You'll have a spiritual reunion as opposed to a physical one.'

'I'm looking forward to seeing Nana Ruth again one day,' discloses Jade.

'So, if there's no heaven or hell, it doesn't seem right that criminals go to the same place as all the good people. Where's the justice in that?' demands Raj.

'We're told in the next world, there are different levels within that world, and the level we attain is based on our faith and our behaviour in this life,' replies Shingo. 'An analogy used is the foetus in the matrix of the womb develops ears, eyes, arms and legs in preparation for this world. Since the next world is a spiritual world of lights, we need to develop virtues like honesty, generosity, kindness, and love in preparation for the next world.'

'In that case, I would imagine a criminal would be the equivalent of a stone in the next world,' reflects Jade.

'That's a great analogy,' responds Shingo. 'Regardless of what level people's souls start off at in the next world, they do progress through the different levels and onto the countless number of worlds for all eternity.'

'I definitely do not want to start at the bottom level, that would be a huge handicap,' comments Raj.

'Oh, and the other thing is, only in this world do we have free will,' explains Shingo. 'Part of our progress in the next world is dependent on God's Mercy. That's why praying for those who have died is important. Prayers assist their souls to continue to progress in the next world.'

'I've been praying and talking to Nana Ruth every night,' reveals Jade. 'I'm glad to hear my prayers will assist her soul to progress. She was such a loving and caring person. I'm sure she entered at a high level, which is why she looked so happy.'

'Yes, I'm sure Nana Ruth started at a high level,' agrees Raj. 'Well, my curfew is 9:00 pm. I better head home.'

'Me, too,' says Jade. 'Thanks again. I'll see you at school on Monday.'

CHAPTER 5

THE EXCURSION

Looking out the window of the school bus, at the tall buildings and slow-moving traffic, Jade exclaims, 'I'm so excited to see the Tutankhamun, Treasure of the Gold Pharaoh.'

'It's the largest and most impressive Tutankhamun exhibition to ever leave Egypt,' comments Raj.

'I'm not a fan of history, but I do find Egyptian history interesting,' states Shingo.

'Yes, I prefer science and technology over history any day,' says Raj.

'Without history, how do we learn where we have come from?' asks Jade.

'True, but what we are told is not necessarily the whole story or in some cases even the truth,' declares Raj.

'Also, the only history we are taught in school is social

and material history, not spiritual. After all, we are spiritual beings having a human experience,' adds Shingo.

'How would they teach us about our spiritual history, when all the different religions can't agree or worse fighting and killing each other?' asks Jade.

'They would teach about Progressive Revelation and how the different world religions contributed to the advancement of civilization,' says Shingo.

'What is Progressive Revelation?' queries Raj. 'I've never heard of it.'

'Me neither', says Jade.

'Progressive Revelation is about how God has sent different Messengers approximately every 500-1000 years to earth, to teach people about God, and how to live in peace and harmony,' states Shingo.

'So why do we have so many different religions, whose followers think their way, is the only way?' quizzes Raj.

'Because each religion of the past, brought new social teachings to suit the society at the time, and previous religions did not have a covenant stating who their successor would be,' explains Shingo. 'That's why there are so many denominations and schisms among the world's previous religions due to disagreement.'

'I remember Nana Ruth used to say, 'Jesus wouldn't even recognise Christianity nowadays',' remarks Jade.

'Give me an example of a social change,' requests Raj.

'Well according to Judaism and Islam, their followers can't eat pork,' states Shingo. 'That's because refrigeration hadn't been invented and people would've become very ill if they ate pork.'

'Well, I don't eat pork because I think pigs are too intelligent to be eaten,' comments Jade.

'What would be an example of a new social teaching nowadays?' asks Raj.

'In the Baha'i Faith, there are no clergy, priests, Imams or Rabbis,' responds Shingo. 'Nowadays more people are literate, and can study the Holy Books and Writings themselves, and decide what they believe.'

'I like the fact, you can find the answers yourself,' muses Jade.

An announcement blares over the bus's intercom, as it approaches the parking bay in front of the museum. Jade, Shingo, and Raj disembark, joining their school group, who are gathering on the left side of the museum's entry at the bottom of the wide staircase.

*****

Peering through the glass at the Egyptian Sarcophagus on display, Jade quizzes, 'Did you know ancient Egyptians removed organs to help preserve the corpses, but they placed them in jars and sealed them in the tomb with the body?'

'Why?' asks Shingo.

'Because they thought they would need them in the Afterlife,' says Jade.

'It says here they always left the heart,' reads Raj. 'Look at this tool they used to remove the brain through the nose.'

'That's gross,' comments Jade. 'Imagine having to embalm a body.'

'They don't remove the organs anymore,' states Raj. 'They drain the blood, release the gases by making small incisions and pump chemicals through the circulatory system.'

'I think, I want to be cremated, and my ashes spread in the mountains or the ocean,' reflects Jade.

'I don't know what I'll do. To be honest. I have not thought about it,' discloses Raj.

'As Baha'is, we can't be cremated,' says Shingo.

'How come?' asks Jade.

'According to real and natural order and Divine law, since the body was developed gradually, it must decompose gradually,' replies Shingo. 'Cremation prevents the combination and mixing of elements back into physical creation.'

'Are there any special rituals about how you prepare and bury the body?' asks Jade.

'Baha'is have to be buried no further than an hour's journey from where they died. The body is wrapped in a shroud of either white cotton or silk fabric,' responds Shingo. 'We don't have any special rituals, but we say the 'Prayer for the Dead' together.'

'I was wondering why ancient Egyptians were buried with artefacts and a 'shabti' doll,' announces Raj. 'It says here, at least one shabti doll was placed in the tomb to serve as one's replacement when called to service by the God Osiris.'

'That's because ancient Egyptians thought the Afterlife was a continuation of their life here on earth,' explains Jade.

'It also says, they believed the soul consisted of nine parts,' reads Raj.

'Kind of reminds me of Lord Voldemort in Harry Potter, how he split his soul into seven parts,' comments Jade.

'Well thankfully our soul is made of one indivisible substance and therefore, eternal,' states Shingo. 'Imagine if it could be split, how weak and vulnerable we would become.'

'Ancient Egyptians obviously believed the soul was still connected to the body after death which is why they used mummification,' suggests Jade.

'So how exactly is our soul connected to our body?' asks Raj.

'According to the Baha'i Writings, interestingly we are told our soul is not in our body,' explains Shingo. 'It has a connection with the body like that of the sun being reflected in a mirror.'

'That being the case, then anything that affects our body, wouldn't affect our soul,' reflects Jade.

'Yes, however, our emotions affect our souls,' responds Shingo.

'So, when I feel sad and miss Nana Ruth, it's my soul grieving,' remarks Jade.

'Yes,' says Shingo.

'Hey, where is the rest of the class? It must be lunchtime,' comments Raj. 'I'm starving.'

'Let's check out the cafeteria,' suggests Jade. 'I hope they have some vegetarian options.'

CHAPTER 6

THE HISTORY PROJECT

During a history lesson the following week, Jade announces, 'I've decided to continue with the Egyptian theme, and learn more about their funeral practices and beliefs about the Afterlife for my project.'

'I wish I could instead look at modern-day practices such as cryopreservation,' comments Raj.

'Isn't that when they decapitate corpses and freeze their heads in some sort of liquid nitrogen?' questions Shingo.

'Well, some people do decide to just freeze their heads. That's called neuro suspension,' replies Raj. 'Others freeze their whole body. And yes, liquid nitrogen is commonly used, as is liquid helium.'

'Sounds like something out of a horror movie,' says Jade. 'I can't comprehend how anyone would want to do such a thing.'

'It's not cheap. The companies that invest in this, are

really taking advantage of people's fear of death,' states Shingo. 'When their souls, transition to the Afterlife, they'll realise they just wasted a lot of money.'

'Well, who knows with the advances in technology,' comments Raj. 'I must admit even though I am so pro-science, I don't want to freeze my body or head.'

'What society or culture are you going to do your project on, Shingo?' asks Jade.

'I'm thinking maybe Indigenous Australians,' responds Shingo. 'They are the oldest living culture on the planet, over 60,000 years old.'

'That would be interesting,' comments Jade.

'Going back to our earlier discussion, the other day, about different Messengers of God being sent and how the social teachings change the society at that time,' reflects Raj. 'In what major ways has religion influenced civilization over the centuries?'

'Moses and Jesus' teachings are about showing loving kindness to your neighbours and those who cross your path,' explains Shingo. 'Muhammad taught about uniting people to form nations and states. Baha'u'llah, the founder of the Baha'i Faith, the latest Messenger of God, teaches about the oneness of humanity and uniting the world.'

'That's very ambitious,' comments Jade. 'Sometimes, I wonder if we'll ever have world peace or end up destroying the planet through a nuclear war.'

'The Baha'i Writings state peace is inevitable, however, things may get worse before they get better until we have true justice and unity in the world,' states Shingo.

'So, we may have a World War III?' asks Raj.

'We might before we have peace,' replies Shingo. 'The choice is up to humanity.'

'I feel like we don't utilise our people power enough,' expresses Jade. 'My parents used to take part in peace marches and rallies when they were younger.'

'Marches nowadays are more about climate change,' comments Raj. 'I think the main concern is our planet may not be habitable in the future, even without a World War III, from all the pollution and overpopulation.'

'There're also marches that pop up about different issues like racism and reconciliation,' adds Jade.

'They're all important - after all, we are all connected to each other and to the earth,' affirms Shingo.

Glancing at his watch, Raj states, 'I'm so glad it's nearly lunchtime, I'm starving.'

'You're always starving,' comments Jade. 'And yet you never seem to gain any weight. Half your luck.'

'It's all in the genes,' replies Raj. 'You guys have to help me think of a topic for my history project during lunch. I really need to start researching.'

'Ok, let's sit next under the Jacaranda next to the water tank,' suggests Shingo, leading the way down the hallway.

THE RUMOUR

The following day Shingo and Raj approach Jade, who is sitting alone under the Jacaranda tree, drawing with a stick in the dirt.

'She doesn't look very happy,' comments Shingo.

'I wonder what's upset her. It's not like her to take off without us and sit by herself,' says Raj.

'Hi, Jade,' greets Shingo, as he and Raj sit down on the grass next to Jade under the shade of the Jacaranda.

'We were wondering where you'd gotten to,' remarks Raj.

'I just needed to be alone,' expresses Jade, focusing on manoeuvring dirt with a stick.

'What happened?' asks Shingo. 'We were waiting outside your Social Science class, but you'd already gone.'

'Nothing, really,' mumbles Jade.

'Seriously, what has upset you so much?' asks Raj.

Averting Shingo and Raj's eyes, Jade sighs, 'It's all over social media.'

'What's all over social media?' queries Shingo.

Thrusting her mobile phone with an open screen into Shingo's hands, she responds, 'Look what they are saying. It just isn't true.'

Jade is boy crazy. She probably has had sex with Shingo and Raj. Watch out she doesn't seduce your boyfriend next.

'What?!' exclaims Shingo.

'Who would write such a thing?!' demands Raj in disbelief. 'Who would even believe such nonsense?'

'You need to report this to the Principal, and have it removed at once,' declares Shingo.

'Yes, Shingo's right,' agrees Raj. 'This is cyberbullying and defamatory.'

'It was such a shock. It's so hurtful. It's not even true and I feel so ashamed,' discloses Jade.

'The person who wrote this should be ashamed for writing such lies,' exerts Shingo.

'What if some of the students believe it?' asks Jade.

'They wouldn't,' responds Raj. 'But if they did, they're not true friends nor worth hanging out with.'

'I think whoever wrote this is actually jealous of you and our friendship,' suggests Shingo. 'Regardless it's a horrible thing to do.'

'Let's go see the Principal before things get out of hand,' asserts Raj.

'Okay,' agrees Jade weakly.

Standing up dusting the dirt and grass off his trousers, Shingo urges, 'Let's sort this out now.'

*****

Accompanying Jade home following the school bell, Shingo reassures her. 'The Principal has contacted Sharon's parents and is making arrangements to have the post removed from social media.'

'I'm glad he's also mentioning the seriousness and consequences of such acts during the school assembly tomorrow, and writing another article in this week's school newsletter,' adds Raj.

'Thank you, for being there for me and encouraging me to see the Principal,' says Jade. 'I'm still in shock and upset, but I do feel better that something is going to be done. It just goes to show, you never really know anyone,' comments Jade. 'I thought Sharon was actually nice and a friend.'

'It's hard to understand the things people do some-times,' says Shingo. 'Now that I know about the dual na-ture of people, it's easier to see how good people can sometimes do bad things. But it's no, excuse.'

'What do you mean by the dual nature of people?' asks Raj. 'As in we all have two sides - like The Incredible Hulk?'

'That's a good example, although not exactly right,' replies Shingo. 'Our dual nature means we have a higher spiritual self and a lower material self. At any moment in your life, you decide which self your actions will come from.'

'Can you give us a couple of examples?' asks Jade.

'I'll use Sharon as an example,' replies Shingo. 'She'd been friendly to you in the past because she was operating from her higher self, practicing friendliness. But when she wrote that terrible lie on social media, she was operating from her lower self because of her feelings of envy and jealousy.'

'That makes sense,' reflects Raj. 'I'm assuming whatever you focus on is the one that becomes stronger and grows.'

'Yes, exactly,' responds Shingo. 'Everyone makes mistakes. What is important is that we learn from them and don't repeat them.'

'There are somethings that people should know are just plain wrong,' asserts Jade.

'Yes, I'm sure after today, Sharon has certainly learned about not writing lies or anything defamatory online,' states Raj.

'It's not just lies that are damaging, even gossiping about things that are true and backbiting are just as damaging,' comments Shingo.

'Remember when we played Chinese whispers in drama last year?' asks Jade. 'That was a good example of how gossiping can change the facts.'

'I wouldn't trust someone who was always backbiting,' reveals Raj. 'I would always be wondering what they were saying behind my back when I wasn't around.'

'There's this quote that I've never forgotten from the Baha'i Writings about how serious backbiting is,' remarks Shingo. 'Breathe not the sins of others so long as thou art thyself a sinner. Shouldst thou transgress this command, accursed wouldst thou be...'

'Accursed is a very strong word,' comments Jade. 'The first part reminds me of the saying, 'when you point a finger at someone, three are pointing back at you'.'

'So true,' agrees Shingo.

'Well, I better head home, I have so much homework tonight,' says Raj.

'Me too,' says Shingo.

'See you guys tomorrow,' calls out Jade as she walks up onto her front steps.

*****

'I'm so glad this week is over, and I can put the whole social media thing behind me,' discloses Jade, walking alongside Shingo and Raj as they exit the school building.

'Yes, and I'm glad Sharon was suspended. It sends a loud and clear message,' comments Raj.

'By the way, did you guys get an invite to Aidan's party this weekend?' asks Shingo.

'Yes,' replies Jade, 'But I don't think I will go.'

'I didn't,' divulges Raj. 'I guess I'm not "popular". I wouldn't be allowed to go anyway my parents don't know Aidan's parents.'

'Why are you thinking of not going?' asks Shingo.

'I overheard Aidan bragging about how his older brother is going to be "supervising" and they are going to get into their parents' alcohol,' replies Jade. 'I'm not interested in drinking. Besides, it's illegal at our age, and if my parents found out, I would be grounded for life.'

'Well, if Aidan's parents aren't going to be there, I definitely wouldn't be allowed either. Plus, I'm not interested in going if they didn't invite Raj, and you aren't going either,' asserts Shingo.

'Did you know that when teenagers drink alcohol they risk potential brain damage for the rest of their lives?' asks Raj.

'I'm not surprised,' responds Shingo. 'I can see why Baha'is can't drink alcohol. Look at all the problems in society caused by alcohol.'

'My parents only drink alcohol on special occasions,' says Jade. 'I will probably try it when I am old enough.'

'I need all of my brain cells, so I can't imagine that I will drink when I'm older,' comments Raj. 'Let's do something fun ourselves on the weekend.'

'Yeah, how about something like a movie, ten-pin bowling or mini-golf at night?' suggests Jade.

'I don't think any good movies are showing at the moment. They aren't released until Boxing Day or after the New Year,' remarks Shingo.

'I like the idea of mini-golf at night,' suggests Raj. 'If it rains, we could go ten-pin bowling instead.'

'Great mini-golf it is,' affirms Jade. 'I'll ask my parents

if they can drop us off. Shingo do you think your parents can pick us up afterward?'

'Yes, I'll ask. I don't think they have anything planned,' replies Shingo. 'Let's have dessert or a milk-shake in the restaurant afterward.'

'You know me when it comes to food,' comments Raj. 'Count me in. I might have both.'

'Sounds like a plan,' says Jade. 'I need to head straight home today. See you guys tomorrow night.'

'Bye, I'll let you know for sure if my parents can bring us home tomorrow,' says Shingo.

'If they can't let me know,' requests Raj, 'Maybe my parents can pick us up.'

THINKING ABOUT THE FUTURE

'Have you guys decided which four elective subjects you want to do next year?' asks Jade outside their Maths classroom on Monday morning.

'Partly,' replies Raj. 'Two were obvious choices – Engineering and Digital Technology since I want to be a Biomedical Engineer.'

'I also picked Digital Technology,' says Shingo. 'My father suggested I do Business Studies.'

'I'm going to do Art, Dance, and Drama,' says Jade. 'I'm contemplating whether to do retail services because it may assist me to get an afterschool job. Although, Media sounds more interesting.'

'Yes, I was thinking about doing Media as well,' mentions Shingo. 'We could all do Media together, that would be fun.'

'It is certainly one of the more appealing out of the remaining subjects,' agrees Raj. 'I'll put Media down for my third option. I'm still stuck on a fourth.'

'Ok, I'll do Media too,' affirms Jade. 'That's my four subjects sorted.'

'I guess I'll do Business Studies, I'm certainly not an Artsy person,' reveals Raj.

'Lucky, you guys will be in three classes together,' comments Jade.

'I think I'll select Music for my fourth subject,' states Shingo. 'I've been thinking about auditioning for the school's Rock Band in my senior years. Maybe by then, I can convince my parents to buy me an electric guitar.'

'That's a great idea,' encourages Jade. 'You play the Bass and Acoustic guitars really well, and you can sing. I'm sure you'd get selected.'

'Jade's right,' agrees Raj. 'You are really good.'

'Thanks, I will,' responds Shingo. 'I enjoy playing and would love to be in a band even after school, but I also need to think of a career. Unlike Raj, I wouldn't have a clue about what I want to do when I finish high school.'

'I'm not sure either, but we have four more years to figure it out,' comments Jade. 'I may even take a 'gap' year and work and travel around Australia if I still don't know what I want to do.'

'I'm thinking of doing a 'youth year of service',' announces Shingo.

'What's that?' asks Raj. 'Sounds like you are going to join the Australian Army Cadets.'

'Yeah, I never figured you as the military type,' comments Jade.

'No,' laughs Shingo. 'I'm not joining the military. It's a term in the Baha'i community we use when a youth takes a year out of their life either after finishing high school or during their university studies and dedicates it to service in their local community or another community anywhere in Australia. Some Baha'i youth even go overseas during this time as a volunteer.'

'That's a good idea,' responds Jade. 'What sort of things do you do as a volunteer?'

'Usually, youth assist with neighbourhood children's classes which focus on the virtues, and with any junior youth activities and any service or socio-economic projects the community has planned,' replies Shingo. 'Really they assist in any way they can and is needed.'

'That sounds like a good idea, especially if you are not sure what you want to do after high school,' comments Raj. 'I'm going straight to university.'

'I'm not sure if I will actually go to university,' discloses Jade. 'I may do an apprenticeship or work and travel.'

'I probably will go to university,' says Shingo. 'The good thing is not many people nowadays work in the same job all of their life. Can you imagine doing the same thing your whole life?'

'No, not really,' answers Jade. 'But if you loved your job, you probably would.'

'Yes,' says Raj. 'I don't see myself working as anything else but a Biomedical Engineer. There will always be advances in technology and I will need to keep learning to keep up to date.'

'That's true,' responds Shingo. 'I guess I need to work out what I'm interested in and good at, besides playing the guitar and singing.'

'You may become a famous singer or guitarist,' suggests Jade.

'The thing is I want to do more with my life,' reflects Shingo. 'I will always have music in my life and play the guitar.'

Glancing behind Shingo, Jade states, 'Mr. Owen is heading this way, we better head inside.'

'Yes, we don't want to end up in the front or back rows,' agrees Shingo. 'He assumes whoever is in the back is up to no good, and he's always questioning those in the front row.'

JY EMPOWERMENT CAMP

'What are you guys up to these summer holidays?' asks Jade as she pulls her untamed wavy red hair up into a ponytail whilst sitting upright on her beach towel.

'The usual,' replies Raj. 'Working on my various science projects in between hanging out with you guys and being dragged around visiting family friends and relatives.'

'I'm going to a Junior Youth Empowerment Camp,' announces Shingo, whilst applying sunscreen. 'I've been meaning to ask you guys if you were allowed, would you like to come?'

'Sounds interesting. What sort of things will you be doing?' questions Jade.

'Lots of different things like art workshops, music, sports, swimming, and team building activities,' answers Shingo. 'The overall purpose is to encourage us to use our talents and develop our virtues to assist our local community through various service projects.'

'Is this a Baha'i camp?' queries Raj.

'There will be some Baha'i youth leaders called 'animators' and other Baha'i teenagers like me attending, but it isn't a Baha'i camp,' responds Shingo. 'There will be other animators and teenagers going, who aren't Baha'is.'

'Where's the camp going to be?' asks Jade.

'In the Darling Downs region,' answers Shingo. 'I can get my parents to send your parents information about the dates, costs, and permission forms if you like.'

'I'll ask,' says Raj. 'Anything to have a break from my annoying younger cousins.'

'I would like to go. Sounds like fun,' expresses Jade. 'I like the idea of getting involved in local service projects.'

'Are you ready to hit the water slide?' urges Raj. 'The queue is getting longer by the minute.'

'Sure,' responds Jade, as she reapplies some zinc sunscreen across her face before speed walking to beat Raj and Shingo to the queue.

*****

'I'm glad your parents agreed to let you both come,' says Shingo, while unloading his sleeping bag and backpack from the boot of the car.

'Me, too,' agrees Jade already loaded up with her

sleeping bag, backpack, pillow, and a medium-sized pink suitcase.

'You look as if you're moving here,' comments Raj, looking down at Jade's pink suitcase.

'Well, I couldn't make up my mind about what to wear, so I brought several options,' replies Jade.

'Thanks, Mum and Dad, for bringing us,' expresses Shingo hugging his parents.

'Yes, thanks,' says Jade.

'Yes, thank you,' adds Raj.

'Have a wonderful time,' says Shingo's mother. 'We're only a phone call away if you need to talk to us.'

'We will see you at the end of the week,' states Shingo's father.

Pointing towards a large building with green cladding, Shingo suggests, 'That looks like the Hall where we check-in.'

'Welcome,' greets one of the animators. 'I'm Matt.'

'Hi, Matt,' responds Shingo. 'These are my friends Jade and Raj.'

'Hi, Jade and Raj,' says Matt. 'If you head to that table to check-in, they will show you which dormitory you are staying in and you can put your gear in there, and come back for some afternoon tea before we start this after-noon's activities.'

'Thanks,' says Shingo.

'This place looks nice,' comments Jade. 'I noticed some pictures of people canoeing on the wall when we came in. I hope we can go canoeing.'

'Yes, I saw some photos that looked like they were doing orienteering,' says Raj. 'That's something I'm good at from when I was in the Boy Scouts.'

'Hello, I'm Layla', greets a young woman in her mid-twenties, with a friendly smile sitting behind a table with a list of names and name badges. 'Over there is Liam and Olivia. They will show you to your dormitories. After you drop off your gear, come back, afternoon tea will be served shortly. You don't want to miss that. The food at this camp is really good.'

'That's a relief,' expresses Raj. 'I brought some snacks just in case.'

'You're always thinking of your stomach,' laughs Jade.

'Hey, I'm a growing teenager,' responds Raj.

'Hi, Olivia and Liam,' introduces Shingo. 'I'm Shingo and this is Jade and Raj. We were told you'd show us to our dormitories.'

'Hi, welcome. You come with me Jade,' invites Olivia. 'Shingo and Raj, you can go with Liam.'

'Where are you from?' asks Olivia leading Jade towards the girl's dormitory.

'I'm from Brisbane,' replies Jade.

'I used to live in Brisbane, it's my hometown,' states Olivia. 'But I moved to Townsville to study. I like it up there, but it's a bit too hot for my liking. Still getting used to it. I go back home for the mid-year and summer holidays.'

'What year are you in?' asks Olivia.

'I just finished Year 8,' replies Jade. 'I heard the work starts to get harder. I'm looking forward to Year 10 and my senior years when I get to select the subjects I want to study.'

'Yes, I remember those days,' recalls Olivia. 'It's even better when you go to university and specialise and study what you really want.'

'Is this your first time at a JY Empowerment camp?' asks Olivia.

'Yes, I'm not a Baha'i, but my friend Shingo is,' replies Jade. 'I like the idea of getting involved in local service projects, and the camp activities sound like fun.'

'This camp isn't just for Baha'is,' comments Olivia. 'It's for any young people wanting to make a difference in their local community. You don't have to wait until you become an adult before you can make a difference or change things.'

'Yes, I agree. That's why I came,' states Jade.

'Well here's the girls' dormitory. Select any bed that doesn't already have any gear on it,' directs Olivia. 'Do you prefer a top or bottom bunk?'

'Definitely, the top,' replies Jade.

'Great, that's sorted,' says Olivia. 'Ready to join your friends for afternoon tea and make some new friends?'

'Yes, that'd be good,' replies Jade.

'These are delicious,' declares Raj, holding up a half-eaten lamington.

'You couldn't even wait,' laughs Jade. Noticing Raj's plate is piled with a lamington, a caramel tart, and a sausage roll, she comments, 'Leave some for me and the others.'

'There's plenty,' responds Raj indicating with his right hand containing the other half of his lamington towards a table covered in plates and platters with an assortment of sweets and savouries.

'Mmm, these are yummy,' comments Jade. 'I do agree with Layla the food here is really good.'

A tall lanky girl, with blonde hair in a pony-tail approaches Jade, Shingo, and Raj. 'Hi, I'm Lua. I don't believe I've met any of you before. I'm from the Sunshine Coast.'

'Sorry, I'd shake your hand, but it's a bit sticky at the moment, or are we still giving each other the 'elbow',' suggests Jade. 'I'm Jade. This is Shingo and Raj. We are from Brisbane and have been friends since kindergarten.'

'Wow, since kindergarten that's a long time,' responds Lua. 'It must be really nice to have been friends for so long.'

'Yes, it is,' affirms Shingo. 'You're lucky you live on the Sunshine Coast being so close to the beach.'

'Yes, I am lucky,' says Lua. 'This is my first time going to a JY Empowerment Camp. I've been looking forward to it. I hope when I return, I can start up a JY group in my community with some of my friends and a couple of the other Baha'i junior youth. Layla you met at the check-in table, has offered to be the animator for our group.'

'That's a good idea,' reflects Jade, turning to Shingo

and Raj. 'We could start up our own JY group when we get back.'

'Yes, and I can then introduce you to a couple of other Baha'i JY in our area that I know, and we can think of what other friends from school we could invite,' suggests Shingo. 'There are a couple of older youth, I also know, who are trained as animators. I can ask if they will help us.'

'Sounds good,' agrees Raj. 'Don't mind me, but I really must have one more of those lamingtons before they disappear.'

A tall broad-shouldered youth, in his early twenties, walks to the back of the hall near the exit and calls out, 'Can I have everybody's attention, please!'

Gradually the sounds of voices throughout the hall reduce to a low murmur. 'Hi, for those of you who don't know me, I'm Zach. I'm one of the youth animators here at the camp. There are six of us. Can all of the youth animators raise your hands so everyone can see who you are?'

'I'd like to call on Layla to explain what we will be doing this afternoon,' introduces Zach as he turns to face Layla standing by his side.

'Hi, everyone!' calls out Layla. 'This afternoon we have organised a range of activities for you to all get to know one another. We will start off with some "icebreakers", followed by some team building activities. These activities include doing an obstacle course, and a scavenger hunt up until dinner time.'

'You will notice on your name tags a coloured dot,' instructs Zach. 'Those are the teams you have been allocated to, for this afternoon's activities and the remainder of the camp. Please head towards the poster on the wall with the same colour as your dot, to meet your other team members.'

'My dot's red,' announces Jade, looking at Shingo and Rajs' tags.

'Mine's green, the same colour as Raj's,' says Shingo. 'I guess we'll catch up with you at dinner time if not during the activities.'

'May the best team win,' declares Raj.

'It's about team-building, not a competition,' reminds Jade.

'Call it what you will,' smiles Raj.

*****

'So how was the camp?' asks Shingo's mother as they are driving back to Brisbane.

'It was really good, even better than I expected,' replies Shingo.

'Yes, it was great,' responds Jade. 'We did so many fun activities, including my favourite - canoeing. And I've made lots of new friends.'

'I especially enjoyed the food,' comments Raj. 'And I really liked the outdoor activities we did for team building and working collaboratively.'

'What did you learn?' asks Shingo's father.

'We completed the first book in the series for the JY Empowerment Program called 'Breezes of Confirmation',' answers Shingo.

'We also planned how we could start up our own JY group in our area, and the sorts of service projects we could organise,' responds Jade.

'What did you learn about confirmation?' asks Shingo's father.

'When you make sincere efforts towards your goals, God will help you. In other words, you will receive confirmation from God,' answers Raj.

'What sort of service projects are you thinking of,' asks Shingo's mother.

'So far we have thought of putting on a concert for the elderly in the aged care home up the road,' replies Jade. 'We're also thinking of beautifying one of their garden beds, so when they sit outside, they'll enjoy looking at the flowers, and birds.'

'I'm sure when we form a JY group and brainstorm ideas with the others, we'll come up with even more ideas,' suggests Shingo.

'That sounds wonderful,' comments Shingo's mother. 'I'm sure the elderly would be very happy and appreciative of your efforts. Sometimes they feel as if people have forgotten about them.'

'Thank you for taking us and picking us up,' expresses Jade.

'Yes, thank you,' says Raj.

'Yeah, thank you, Mum and Dad,' says Shingo. 'If you

don't mind though, I'm so tired, I just need to "rest" my eyes.'

Yawning, as if on cue, Jade states, 'Yes, I must admit I didn't sleep much last night. We stayed up late talking. Being our last night the animators weren't as strict about our curfew.'

All eyes turned to Raj, who was already sound asleep with a slight smile on his face.

DISCUSSION QUESTIONS

Note: Additional information can be found from The Independent Investigator Series. The Independent Investigator is referred to as I, and The Independent Investigator II is referred to as II.

Chapter 2 – Exploring the Island

1. What are spirit forces?
2. What spirit force do humans possess? (I p. 27)
3. What are the four spirit forces of the physical world?
4. Why is the harmony of science and religion important?

Chapter 3 – The Wake

1. What is one of the proofs of the soul? (I p. 15)
2. What is a *déjà vu* experience? (I p. 15)
3. What happens when we die? (II p.p. 25, 29-30)
4. Is there a heaven and hell? (I p. 31)

5. How many worlds are there in the Afterlife? (I p. 18)

Chapter 4 – Pizza & Movie Night

1. How can we assist loved ones' souls to progress in the Afterlife? (II p.p. 23-24)
2. Where is the Afterlife? (I p. 20)
3. What is the Afterlife like? (I p.p. 21, 24)
4. How will family and friends recognise you in the Afterlife? (II p. 33)

Chapter 5 – The Excursion

1. What is Progressive Revelation? (II p.p. 16, 68)
2. What is a covenant?
3. Why doesn't the Baha'i Faith have clergy, priests, or religious leaders?
4. Why can't Baha'is be cremated? (II p.p. 38-39)
5. How is the soul connected to the body? (I p. 17)

Chapter 6 – The History Project

1. How has religion in the past influenced civilization?

2. What is Baha'u'llah, the founder of the Baha'i Faith's, main mission?
3. Will we ever have peace in this world? (I p.p. 71,73)
4. Will there be a World War III? (I p. 77)

Chapter 7 – The Rumour

1. Can you provide an example of when you have been choosing to act from your higher spiritual self and from your lower material self?
2. What do the Baha'i writings say about backbiting?
3. How does your school deal with cyberbullying?
4. Can Baha'is drink alcohol? Find out what the Baha'i writings say about drinking alcohol. (I p. 50)
5. What are some of the problems caused in society by alcohol?

Chapter 8 – Thinking About the Future

1. What electives have you selected or are thinking of choosing?
2. What are you good at?

3. What do you think you may want to do for work when you grow up?
4. Will you take a gap year or do a Youth Year of Service after high school?

Chapter 9 – JY Empowerment Camp

1. What is the overall purpose of Junior Youth Empowerment Camps?
2. What is an animator?
3. What virtues do junior youth develop whilst participating in the JY Empowerment programs?
4. When do we receive confirmation from God?
5. What ideas do you have for a service project?

BIBLIOGRAPHY

Bahá'u'lláh, *The Hidden Words*, No. 27 From the Arabic, Special Ideas, USA, 1994.

Lemon, T., *The Independent Investigator*, Sacred Square Publishing, Australia, 2019.

Lemon, T., *The Independent Investigator II*, Sacred Square Publishing, Australia, 2019.

https://www.ancient.eu/Egyptian_Burial/

https://www.bbc.com/future/article/20140821-i-will-be-frozen-when-i-die

https://nomadsworld.com/stargazing-australia-new-zealand/

https://www.space.com/four-fundamental-forces.html

https://adf.org.au/talking-about-drugs/parenting/

https://www.health.qld.gov.au/news-events/news/the-effects-of-alcohol-on-the-adolescent-brain

www.ingramcontent.com/pod-product-compliance
Lightning Source LLC
Chambersburg PA
CBHW070401120726
47909CB00008B/2946